AMAMBRE, THE KING FROM THE JUNGLE

Anthony Ansah

To my family and friends.

CHAPTER ONE
AMAMBRE

King Amambre was the King of Esuekyir and its environs. He was such a kind and wise King. Ruling for forty years, King Amambre had gained popularity across his province and beyond. He was the only King in Ghana who had set up a development fund for his town. He had also been praised by many for developing a special community for widows. Kunase was a small community where King Amambre kept all widows to be sheltered, fed and given free medical care.

King Amambre had been elected the President of the National House of Chiefs of Ghana for many years. Unfortunately, there were some of his subjects who resented the King very much. They thought he was not the legitimate heir of the Esuekyir Kingdom. They did not only find fault with everything he did, they also made many attempts to assassinate him. But the King's admirers were more than his oppressors. He had always received information about those evil plots, and had 'armed' himself to defeat his killers. At an international gathering of Chiefs and Kings of Africa one day, Ebusuapanyin Ekuntan narrated the history and the mystery behind King Amambre's enstoolment.

AMAMBRE'S FOREBEARERS ARE TAKEN SLAVES

Esuekyir was a town located behind the Pra River between the Western and Central Regions of Ghana. The early settlers of the town had fought many battles before settling there. It was located on a hill, and the major route to the town was the River Pra. The *forefathers* of Esuekyir believed that the area across the river was the safest place to live. Enemies who wanted to *invade* their community would have to cross the River Pra before getting access to the community, by which time the community members would have attacked and defeated the supposed *captors*. This strategy made Esuekyir a very strong village. The chief of the town, Nana Ekuntan, was a very proud chief. He had defeated many invaders who sought to attack them.

Once there was a fierce battle between Esuekyir and a nearby town, which had always sought to capture them, and make all its *inhabitants* their subjects. Though Esuekyir was smart, the people of Ampa were smarter. The chief of Ampa had sent a spy to settle at Esuekyir for a while to study, and help them *play to their weaknesses*. The spy finished his work successfully and reported to the chief of Ampa, who devised a very clever strategy to fight Esuekyir. Ampa sent their best swimmers to the war, knowing that they had to cross the River Pra before they could invade Esuekyir. The swimmers swam quietly across the river, attacking and killing the three guards at the bank of the river.

Those guards were the people who always blew the loud horn to *alert* the entire Esuekyir of any *imminent* danger. Though they killed a few people, the people of Ampa had to run for their lives when the specially kept 'war dogs' were released by the people of Esuekyir to attack them. The 'war dogs' were released only when a battle had become so *fierce*. Each household had its own 'war dog'. Most of the attackers of Esuekyir were *devoured* by the war dogs. This information spread across all the communities in the area.

Esuekyir became a very powerful community. People from other communities who were in good terms with them ran to them for safety when they were in danger. Such people then became their subjects, they were given some strict *principles* to observe. Foreigners who had come to Esuekyir had to take ten per cent of their farm produce to the chief of Esuekyir annually. Their men and women were *forbidden* from marrying the people of Esuekyir. When a man from a foreign land had any sexual *intimacy* with a woman from Esuekyir, such a man was put to death and the woman was banished from the community. Young ladies who had reached the puberty stage had to be *initiated* into womanhood. Those ladies went through *rigorous* examination by an elderly woman from the palace to ensure that they had not had any sexual intercourse before the puberty rites.

Ladies from Esuekyir community who were found guilty were *banished* from the town whilst those from foreign communities were executed outrightly. Customs and traditions were observed to the letter at Esuekyir. Many *taboos* guided the conduct of people in and outside the community. People who dared those taboos suffered dearly for their deeds. Christianity wasn't known to the people at that time so they depended only on lesser deities for all the solutions to their problems, and for answers to some *paranormal phenomena*. This, however, worked for them. There was orderliness in the community at that time.

Nyamewa's parents were taken *captive* by the people of Esuekyir in a battle that *ensued* between Esuekyir and Apow. Her mother was pregnant with Nyamewa during the war. Both she and her husband suffered severe injuries during the fierce battle. When they were taken to Esuekyir, Nyamewa's father, Kwadwo Anim, couldn't do any had work.

He had lost one arm during the war, and had also *sprained* his right leg. He couldn't therefore, work very hard to give much supply to the chief during the annual ten per cent food supply to the palace. That had attracted some hatred from the chief. Nyamewa's mother *passed away* shortly after her birth. That was due to the severe injury she sustained during the battle. Nyamewa was therefore *catered for* by her father.

It was a real difficult time raising Nyamewa as her father did everything with one arm. With great difficulty, Kofi Anim, *took care of* Nyamewa *single-handedly*. He did all he could to provide the needs of his daughter.

Nyamewa grew into a very pretty girl. She stood tall among all her peers. She had received good training from her father. Nyamewa's qualities were *unquestionable*. She was selfless, down to earth, and very empathetic. Kofi Anim had taught her daughter all the norms of Esuekyir. Nyamewa knew all the *dos and don'ts* of the community in which she lived.

Education at that time was not very popular among girls. Nyamewa was therefore put into *apprenticeship* when she turned sixteen. Many young men, some of whom were *native* Esuekyir people had expressed interest in Nyamewa, but, she paid deaf ears to all those submissions. She, however, did that politely, in order not to offend anyone.
The chief's son was among the men who were interested in Nyamewa. Ohenkan, the prince, had gained *notoriety* for his uncontrolled affection for young ladies.

Though he was in his late thirties, all attempts by his father to make him marry had failed. Being the prince, many young ladies naturally had interest in him. Most of those expressions were *undoubtedly*, mere *infatuations*. No serious lady would want to settle with a man like Ohenkan, if not for his wealth, power and fame. Those ladies who themselves *admired* Ohenkan were not spared at all. That, however, did not satisfy him. He wanted to *have his way* with any lady he *came across*. He particularly showed interest in ladies who proved 'stubborn'. He would go any length to get such ladies, and after, *embarrass* them.

During one of his usual walks through the community, Ohenkan *bumped into* Nyamewa. He quickly made some enquiries about her, and realised that Nyamewas was from Apow, a rival community his father had conquered some years ago. He was interested in Nyamewa, and would even want her for a wife, but, their customs and traditions forbade him from marrying a 'slave'. This was a *genuine* affection Ohenkan had for Nyamewa. "What would I do? How do I get this pretty and *well-mannered* lady to marry. This is a real woman who is cut out, in all respects, for queenship, but tradition won't permit me to have her. How awful could customs be, sometimes!" Ohenkan fumed. He decided to approach Nyamewa with his 'request'.

The following day, Ohenkan sent for Nyamewa secretly and informed her about his desire to settle with her. This was the first time Ohenkan had respectfully expressed interest in a young lady. He was however shocked by the quick and *unequivocally* negative response that came from Nyamewa. "No, please, I can't *flout* the traditions of this land in anyway. A prince of your calibre should know better. My family and I have had enough suffering, please, let *me be,* " *lamented*, Nyamewa. Ohenkan felt some cold blood move through his veins when Nyamewa *sternly* refused his proposal. He was speechless. Nyamewa left the Prince's presence without any *hesitation.* Ohenkan got sick, he was completely *disorganised.* He didn't want to *disclose* his feelings to his father because it was abominable even to have such a discussion with his strict father. He thought of forcing his way with Nyamewa but he was also scared of the *consequences.* He loved Nyamewa, and did not want any harm to *befall* her. "If I do anything *untoward* with Nyamewa, she would be banished from Esuekyir. I can't watch this to happen to such an *innocent* lady like Nyamewa, " he *contemplated*. Ohenkan was in a cleft stick for many weeks. He wished he could change those long, *unyielding dogmas*.

After much *contemplation*, Ohenkan decided to have a healthy discussion with Nyamewa's father concerning his *affection*. He paid a visit to Kofi Anim, whose daughter had already informed him about the matter. Though Kofi Anim had lent some ears to Ohenkan, his response was just like his daughter's. He had not forgotten the trauma Ohenkan's father had caused his family and his entire community. He did not only want to observe tradition, he also didn't want to have anything to do with the Chief of Esuekyir and all his regales. Ohenkan was embarrassed. He was old enough to understand the expression on Kofi Anim's face that suggested total dislike for all members of his family . He went home completely *under a cloud.* He was *distraught .*

Ohenkan met Nyamewa at the market one day, and continued to *negotiate* with her. This time, Nyamewa flew into passion. She didn't understand why the prince would want to disrespect his own traditions, and put her into such a *dilemma.* "Even if tradition permitted such a relationship, I would not marry you ; your family killed my mother, and injured my father. Until now, we're your slaves. To *pour oil into flames*, you don't have manners. You don't respect women, I'm not interested in fame, nor wealth for marriage. I want a decent man to marry, and make good impact on my community." Nyamewa flared up.

After much reflection without any way out, Ohenkan decided to *take the rough with the smooth*. One night he went out on a special mission to have his way with Nyamewa. He went to sit somewhere in the dark at the outskirts of the town, and sent his two assistants to fetch Nyamewa for him. Nyamewa had gone to the night market to buy kerosene. When she was returning home, Ohenkan's assistants monitored her, and *kidnapped* her, covering her face with a piece of cloth tied to her nape. They took her straight to Ohenkan's *hideout*, and dumped her helplessly before the prince.

Ohenkan raped Nyamewa and went his way. Nyamewa, who was *unconscious* all this while, woke up to see the prince, almost *through with* her. Words could not explain the shock, disappointment, and the pain that were registered in Nyamewa's heart. At age eighteen, she was determined never to have *affair* with any man until she was duly married. "What offence have my family and I committed against Ohenkan and his family? They invaded my village, killed and injured many people, including my parents, and took the surviving ones as slaves. Now, Ohenkan has *ruined* my life too. Why? Why is nature this unfair?" Nyamewa wept, as she tottered home.

She *narrated* the whole ordeal to her father, who went straight to the chief's palace. "Nana, your son has raped my daughter. She is at home right now, weeping *uncontrollably*." reported Kofi Anim. The chief didn't believe what Kofi Anim said. He was fast at reasoning. "How could you come here alone if indeed your daughter had been raped?" he quizzed. "Throw this hungry man out of the palace." He ordered. Kofi Anim was quickly sent out of the palace by the palace guards.

Kofi and his daughter were *at their wit's end* in dealing with their plight. They were slaves, and there was no way they could win a case against an ordinary citizen, let alone, the chief and his son.

CHAPTER TWO
AMAMBRE'S MOTHER IS BANISHED FROM ESUEKYIR

Two months later, Nyamewa was found pregnant. Unfortunately, she was yet to go through the *rigorous* puberty rites, which would be due in a week's time.

The day came for all the young ladies at puberty to be examined for the *bragor*. The old lady, as usual, assembled all the girls and inspected them. It got to Nyamewa's turn, and the experienced old lady immediately identified that Nyamewa had taken seed. She was marched straight to the palace to meet the chief. Kofi Anim, who was *anxious* about all the *proceedings*, decided to follow his daughter into the palace. "Nana, this girl is pregnant. She can't undertake the *initiation* into *adulthood*. Please, let tradition deal with her," explained the old lady. "Who are you, and who impregnated you?" asked the chief. Nyamewa was *courageous*. She was ready for the worst. "I am a slave, from Apow and this is my father. I was raped and impregnated by Ohenkan, the prince." said Nyamewa boldly. There was loud silence when Nyamewa spoke. The chief looked at Kofi Anim, and quickly remembered a day he had reported a rape case to him. At that moment, the chief ordered everyone to leave the scene except Nyamewa and her father. " Are you sure of what you are saying?" *queried*, the chief. " I hope you know the *consequences* of what you have done. If I investigate and ascertain that you are telling lies, your woes will just be *compounded* " warned the chief.

The chief sent Nyamewa and the father home so he could ask Ohenkan about the veracity of Nyamewa's story. The chief asked his son, and it was *established* that, Ohenkan was the one responsible for Nyamewa's pregnancy. What made the act so *grievous* was that, Ohenkan actually raped Nyamewa, an act that was *forbidden* on that land. "We all know the gravity of the offence you have committed. Let's be smart here, " *whispered*, the chief to his son. We shall all appear before the people, but when you're asked, deny *vehemently*. Stress that you are *innocent,* and that the girl only seeks to *embarrass* you so as to have her way into your fame and wealth. Let them know that, as the prince of the land, you are not *oblivious* of the traditions that had been passed down by your forefathers. It would therefore be impossible to commit such as act, given the thousands of ladies who willingly admire you. I will then make an *inescapable* case against them, so we could get off the hook, " *concocted,* the chief and his son.

Though Ohenkan was not very comfortable with the *repercussions* that were about to hit Nyamewa, there was nothing he could do. He couldn't have put himself into any *damning* situation by refusing what his father had suggested. "But, Daddy, can't we do anything to invalidate traditions and taboos, especially when they have adverse effects on the citizenry? Asked, Ohenkan feebly. " What are we repealing tradition for? Do you know how many crimes you have committed here? You have raped, made a slave pregnant, and what's worse! She was pregnant before puberty rites. And who committed all these, the prince, the custodian of the traditions of the land. Do you know the punishments for all these crimes?" The chief said with much *fury* in his eyes.

The following day, the chief invited Kofi Anim and his daughter to his palace, together with all the elders of the community. "You are all welcome, my elders. We all know the issue at stake. This lady here has accused the prince of raping and impregnating her before her puberty rites. As we all know, this act invites grave consequences on both the woman and the man. The situation is more *precarious* when the act occurs between a foreigner and a native member of the town. We are here therefore, to find the truth of the matter," narrated the chief.

After this, Ohenkan was asked to respond to the *allegation*. "You all know my status in this community. I've been trained strictly by the traditions of our land in order to conveniently take over from my father. It will therefore be very strange for me to *drag the traditions of the land through the mud* by committing such an *abominable* act. Also, I am the prince, and by the virtue of my position, I won't struggle to get a woman, even if I want. I don't go after women, women come after me. How possible could it be then, that I would *stoop so low* as to rape a slave for that matter? If I wanted this lady, I would go for her the right way, and not by this *unacceptable* act. I believe it's a well planned attempt by this man and his daughter, to embarrass me, my father, and to bring the whole throne into *disrepute*. They should be given the highest form of punishment because they have already *traduced* the whole kingdom by plotting such a crime against the prince." Ohenkan said *explicitly*. He sounded very *plausible* but that was *specious*. Nyamewa, who couldn't control her tears, could not utter a word when she was called for her side of the story. She was *drenched* in tears. Her father, who was also *dumbfounded* by the great *ingenuity* with which the prince lied, couldn't help but to burst into uncontrollable tears. "Apply all necessary sanctions on the lady, and execute this man for *denigrating* the entire stool, " ordered the chief.

Nyamewa's father was killed, and Nyamewa was banished from Esuekyir. Both punishments were executed at night. After watching her father being killed, Nyamewa was taken to an unknown *destination* in a thick forest with her eyes tied. Even when morning had arrived, it was difficult to see in the forest. The big trees, with the thick tiers, had created so much shade which had made the forest dark. " Why will I have to go through this agony? What offence did I commit? Oh, dear mother nature, if indeed you are, then *avenge* me." Nyamewa *grieved*. Her grief was too much to explain in words.

Nyamewa preferred to die like her *predecessors*, than to suffer those *atrocities*. "Where am I? Where will I get food and water to survive?" she *sobbed*. She was *hiccupping* from too much weeping. Nyamewa wept till she slept. Whilst she was asleep, she felt something very slippery on her leg. She woke up quickly to see that, a very big python had almost swallowed one of her legs. But for the fact that her legs were a few centimeters apart, the python would have swallowed her whole. Having gone through series of dangerous *escapades*, the sight of the python didn't even frighten her that much. She picked the small knife that had been used to stab her father multiple times to death, and gradually bisected the python from the mouth to the tail. She freed herself from the python, but she was not free.

Nyamewa stayed in the forest for months, eating wild fruits and drinking the dew that formed on the leaves as water. She had become a jungle lady. She heard strange noises that sounded like humans' but she saw no one around. Being *immune* to fear, Nyamewa didn't care anymore what happened to her in the forest. She wandered for very long distances but didn't seem to escape from the forest, neither did she come across anybody. She rested on leaves when she was too tired to travel any further.

CHAPTER THREE
AMAMBRE IS BORN

One day, she slept after roaming for a very long time, and woke up to find herself in the hut of a very old woman. She had never met the old woman before, but, she looked harmless. The old woman who strangely knew Nyamewa's name, boiled some water with some herbs, and applied oh her feet to *exhume* the thorns which had entered her skin. This was very painful though, but Nyamewa *endured* all. Parts of her feet were decaying from the piercing of sharp thorns into her skin. She had also suffered other injuries from insect bites. Nyamewa had also grown very lean. She had not had any good food to eat apart from the wild fruits. After treating her, the old lady fed her, and gave her some *concoction* that put her into a deep sleep. She felt much healthier and more relieved when she woke up.

Life with the old lady was more comfortable. Though Kofi Anim had raised Nyamewa with love, the latter had never received such treatment as was given by the old lady. She didn't have to stress herself before getting food to eat. The old lady seemed to know much about Nyamewa. She however, didn't disclose her *identity* to Nyamewa. "You are such a kind woman. You have saved me from death. You feed me, and you shelter me, please, who are you?" Nyamewa sought to know the old lady, who didn't utter any word. There was something very strange about the old lady. She was not seen going to the forest for any game or fruits, but, there was always food to eat. She readily served Nyamewa when she perceived that she was hungry. She didn't have to ask but, the old lady herself was never seen eating any food. Though these things marveled Nyamewa, she didn't worry about them because she could obtain all her basic needs from the old lady.

Throughout her stay with the old lady, there was no *verbal* interaction between the two. She was still pregnant and her time was almost due for labour. One day, the old lady went to a nearby stream to fetch water. Nyamewa quietly followed her to see if she could find anything to satisfy her curiosity about the old lady. But, at the bank of the stream, Nyamewa couldn't see the old lady anymore. She could only see the gourd which the old lady was going to use to fetch water. She then decided to swim in the stream whilst she waited for the old lady. When she took off her clothes, and entered the stream, a very heavy rainstorm started suddenly. It rained heavily with lightning flashing violently in the sky. Soon, the stream had overflowed its banks, eroding even the heavy *logs* in its *catchment*.

Nyamewa was struggling to breath as the rushing water swept her away helplessly. She held a small tree and tried to pull herself out of the stream but the tree was too weak for the weight of a pregnant woman like Nyamewa. It broke and Nyamewa was seen rolling *randomly* in the raging stream.   The old lady was nowhere to be found. She appeared to be aware of all that was happening. She knew it was taboo for a pregnant woman to swim in a river, and that she couldn't do anything about the *aftermath* of such acts. Unfortunately, Nyamewa was not aware of any such taboo, lest, she'd not flout it. It was very strange that the forces behind taboos could not save innocent people from the effects of breaking them. The sudden rain *subsided* and the old lady walked *downstream* to check where Nyamewa might be. Under one big tree at the bank of the river, the old lady could hear the cry of a newly born baby which had not completely come out of the mother. Nyamewa had passed away during delivery. The old lady raced against time to save the baby. With her experience, she knew what to do to keep the baby alive. She didn't worry much about Nyamewa as there was *no need to cry over spilled milk*. She bathed the baby and milked some *colostrum* from her sheep which was also about to give birth for it. For three months, Nyamewa's baby *fed on* the breast milk from the sheep. After that period, there was no more milk from the sheep as the sheep had *weaned* its lambs. The old lady had no other option than to give the baby mashed yam with palm nut oil.

The boy grew up and the old lady named him Amambre, which literary meant ' Traditions'. The old lady *coined* Amambre's name from the evil traditions that had been followed for *centuries*, and had destroyed many lives, including that of his mother, Nyamewa. She took pains to educate the boy about his root, and all the *adventures* that brought his existence. Though it was very hard to believe the old lady, Amambre didn't have any *counter* information. He had to accept what he had been fed with. He wondered how a mere tradition could let his father banish his mother from their community without considering what might happen to her. He had no practical experience of wars, and thus did not actually understand the practice of slavery which brought his mother and father together.

The story looked even more *spurious* to him when the old lady told him that she was not part of his family *lineage*, and that she was only *mandated* to ensure his upkeep and safety. Not even the sight of his mother's grave which the old lady had showed Amambre could convince him fully. He only knew the old lady as his mother, and hoped to see the reality of all that he had been told someday.

Amambre turned seventeen, and he really looked like a man. He was well-built, and had hair all over his skin. No animal could escape from his hunting skills if he saw it. Sometimes, he used his bare hands to *strangle* some wild animals. Amambre was a very strong boy.

One day, he observed something. He perceived that he was completely different from the old lady. He then started reflecting on all the stories the old lady had told him. He had made those observations from some mating and delivery scenes he had beheld in the forest. Amambre observed that some animals mated, and in no time, they conceived. After sometime, the female gave birth, and had *offspring* walking after it. "If it is the same among humans, then my story might be true. " he *reasoned*. Amambre wanted to know more. He asked the old lady series of questions about his supposed root. The old lady, who was talking at that time, was elated. She knew that day would definitely come for Amambre to " gain *consciousness* ". She gladly taught Amambre all that he needed to know. "If I ever come into contact with the *perpetrators* of those *heinous* acts in the name of traditions, I would tear them apart." Of course, some of the taboos are meaningful, and could be used to check human behaviour in the communities, but, they should all serve the interest of the people.

Traditions should be established for societal good. Traditional laws shouldn't invite misery and agony unto its subjects. Why should a whole human being be killed for getting pregnant before puberty rites, when the pregnancy itself would bring another human being? When we put the pregnant girl to death, two lives have been lost. Will this not affect the society? Can't life continue after pregnancy?

The taboos must be reasonable. There should be a more *constructive* punishment other than killing or banishment and there should be much education to avoid such occurrences if we are very serious about it." Amambre reasoned. He wondered why nature itself didn't see anything wrong by making a young lady 'mature' at that stage, but, mere human beings could take the lives of such people when they committed such *misdemeanor.* Amambre, however, *admonished* that pre-marital sex was a very bad practice, and that proper mechanisms should be used to address the situation rather than killing and banishment. He was very successful in his education. The old woman watched Amambre with great delight as she observed much wisdom in the boy's *propositions.*

CHAPTER FOUR
AMAMBRE LEAVES FOR ESUEKYIR

At eighteen years, Amambre was old enough to rule his people. One day, he informed the old lady to direct him to his father's land. "I want to kill all those murderers. I want to take over the throne, and correct all the mess that have been created over the years." he revealed. "No, Amambre, killing isn't the best way to go.

If you want to save a situation, use a very clever way to do it. You could sit, and *dialogue* with your fathers. Explain to them the need to *abolish inhuman* traditional practices. Educate them on how important human life is. They'll understand. Even if they don't, you could wait till your time to rule, then you could change things" said the old lady. Amambre understood. There was complete sense in the old lady's submission. "But Mummy, I don't think they'll listen to me or that; they'll ever make me rule. What do I do then?" asked Amambre. " If you still face strict *opposition* after several attempts to handle the matter peacefully, then the only option is to fight. But, don't fight to kill, just fight to render the antagonist *ineptitude* so that you could carry out your objectives. It's a really difficult task to effect change in a society. Many people have died in the process of trying to change some *misconceptions*. Sometimes, the whole society might stand against you, but, as a leader, you must be bold and *resilient*, you'll succeed, " responded the old lady.

Amambre was set to go. The old lady gave him her *benediction*. Amambre took a small knife the old lady gave him as an *inheritance* from his mother, some cola nuts, and two eggs. He also took with him some *shire* - white clay. He kept those items in a small sack and left.

"Be very careful on the way, follow the path straight without any turn. You'll cross three large rivers, be careful not to spit, nor urinate into any of them. Do not forget to smear your skin with cola nut before crossing the second river. Do not express fear about tackling any difficulty that might come your way, but, use wisdom in everything you do, you'll succeed," instructed, the old lady.

Amambre set off. He walked a very long distance, and came across the first river. At a distance, he could hear the roar of a beast. As he *approached* the bank of the river, the roar of the beast became louder and louder. Amambre stopped and pondered for a while; two main instructions were *reverberating* on his mind. "Do not express fear,...use wisdom...".

Amambre realised that meeting the beast face-to-face could be very deadly. He therefore decided to climb a tall tree to *catch a glimpse of* the beast before taking the next action. As a jungle man, he had no difficulty climbing trees. He quickly climbed a very tall tree to look at the supposed beast. As if he knew, he saw a figure that was *commensurate* with the roar he heard. There was a huge, black hairy figure that stood upright like a man. It was a real giant monster, which looked very hungry and wild. Its height was about 1.8m with width 60cm. Amambre remembered the stories about some wild beasts the old lady had told him. According to the old lady, those wild beasts occasionally invaded human communities and devoured many people when after many months, they had not got anything to feed on. They mostly lived in mangrove forests. Amambre had to devise a quick plan to get rid of the beast so he could continue his journey. "I can't kill this monster. I can only divert its attention from the bank of the river, so I could cross."

Amambre thought. He climbed down and caught a monkey. Amambre tied one leg of the monkey to a tree far from the bank of the river with a very long vine. The distance was about 200m from the bank of the river. He then climbed the tree again, hid in the branches and left the monkey to fall a few metres behind the monster. Upon hearing the sound from the fallen monkey, the beast turned and pursued the monkey. Amambre quickly jumped into the river when he had climbed down to the middle of the tree, and swam across the river. The beast heard the *splash* made by Amambre's fall into the water and diverted its attention back to where the sound came from.

When it *darted* back to the bank of the river, Amambre, who heard the beast approach the river side, was swimming underwater. Funnily, the monkey also got to where it had been tied, and *squealed* loudly because it couldn't free itself. This sound diverted the attention of the beast again from the bank of the river. At this time, Amambre swam to the bank across the river. He was safe, but, very tired. He moved a bit farther from the river and decided to rest under a tree.

When he woke up, he saw himself surrounded by some short creatures who were playing drums. He had *apparently* rested under the tree where dwarfs usually met to play. Again, he remembered a story the old lady had told him about dwarfs. According to the old lady, dwarfs were not harmful creatures but they loved to 'capture' humans. They usually captured humans and stayed with them for years. During this period, they would play with the person during the day, and train the person in the use of herbs in the evening.

Amambre was told that dwarfs slept only for two hours, from 12 am to 2 am. People who were captured and released by dwarfs became great herbalists in many communities, according to the old lady. The old lady informed Amambre that great priests such as Okomfo Anokye, Togbui Tsali and Okomfo Damoa, who found cure for many spiritual and physical diseases, were all people who had once been captured by dwarfs. But, Amambre wasn't ready to become a herbalist. His encounter with the old lady, and his long period of stay in the forest had exposed him to some *considerable* knowledge in *herblore* and *herbalism*. He therefore had to find a way to escape from the dwarfs so he could to pursue his mission. Amabre knew that dwarfs hated *shire*. When a person smeared white clay on himself, the one could not be seen by dwarfs.

After playing with Amambre the whole day, the chief dwarf rubbed his palm on Amambre's lips, and Amambre suddenly became full and strong. At midnight when the dwarfs had slept, Amambre ground some *shire (white clay), and* rubbed his whole body with it.

Early the following morning, Amambre got up and walked quietly away. Though he could see the dwarfs awake, the short creatures couldn't see Amambre walk away.

Amambre continued his journey to Esuekyir, a town he had never stayed in before, but had been told a lot about. After walking another long journey, he came across the second river. He didn't know why the old lady told him to smear his body with cola nuts before crossing the second river, but, he did. The second river was not as deep and wide as the first one. Unlike the first river which reached his chest, the second river was only at his knee. Amambre therefore thought he could cross the river with much ease, but, he was wrong.

When he had crossed the river to the middle, he felt 'something' grip his leg firmly. Suddenly, the 'thing' started pulling him upstream very fast. Initially, Amambre was scared, but, when he remembered the instruction, "do not express fear in any difficulty that might come your way", and how he fiercely defeated some wild animals in the forest, Amambre decided to battle the crocodile. He used his knife to stab the croc at the back, but, the cut was very small due to the hard skin of the crocodile. Amambre then heard a soft voice in his ear to rub some cola nuts in the cut. When he applied the cola nut in the cut, the crocodile left Amambre's leg and started turning itself violently in pain. Amambre quickly crossed the river and sat at the bank to watch the crocodile tumble in the river in pain. After a while, the water became calm, and Amambre saw the crocodile float on the river. It was dead.

Amambre then applied some 'acheampong' herbs on his wound, and rested for a while. After taking enough rest, Amambre continued his journey.

He walked for a whole day but couldn't reach the last river, after which he would be getting to Esuekyir, according to the old lady. He could, however, hear some drumbeats from a very far end. His hopes were fulfilled as he heard the drumbeats for he knew he was close to home. Amambre came across some pawpaws and sighed in relief as he had starved for days.

He quickly plucked some of the pawpaws and sat down to eat. After eating, he decided to rest for a while before he continued his journey. Whilst he was resting, the weather suddenly became dark, threatening to rain. A heavy thunderstorm began. The rain was so heavy that in no time, the whole place where Amambre rested, was flooded. Amambre didn't know what to do. There was no hill nearby, and the rain was still pouring as if a dam had overflowed. The water level at where Amambre was had reached his waist, and was rising quickly. Soon, the water reached Amambre's neck, and the heavy *current* swept him away.

Poor Amambre employed all his swimming skills to free himself from the flooding, but, he seemed to have no headway. This time, all his brevity, wisdom and strength had 'disappeared'. He was between life and death. Amambre quickly *recalled* a story the old lady had told him about the *bizarre* manner through which his mother passed away. He admitted that it might be his destiny to also 'depart' in a similar manner. Whilst he was struggling in the water, Amambre prayed to the ancestors to rescue him as he knew he had started the end of his life. After a loud cry, Amambre blacked out.

CHAPTER FIVE
AMAMBRE REACHES ESUEKYIR

Amambre *resuscituted* suddenly to see himself surrounded by some armed men. He didn't quite understand what was happening because he had not seen such a crowd before in his entire life. Whilst some of the men raced against time to restore his life, others were watching carefully to prevent any *ambushment*.

The warriors of Esuekyir had all been informed to be on their toes as they had not seen such a well-built, hairy and handsome man like Amambre before. Amambre regained consciousness but could not talk immediately because he was very weak. He was *sandwiched* straight to the **Ahemfie**, the chief's palace, and interrogated.

Amambre's grandfather had died, and had been succeeded by Ahenkan, Amambre's father.

He was interrogated after he had been greeted with some hospitality. The *sumptuous* meal from the royal house made Amambre really feel at home.

''I don't know my mother. But, I know of an old lady who told me all about my mother, and my root. She gave me the name Amambre, because she said all my agony *stemmed* from bad traditions. According to the old lady, my mother's name was Nyamewa. She was captured and made a slave at Esuekyir. Whilst there, the prince of the land, Ahenkan, got her pregnant but denied responsibility.

She was therefore banished from the community when she was found pregnant before her puberty rites. Her father, Kofi Anim, was killed because according to the chief, he and his daughter had conspired to denigrate the reputation of the entire stool by accusing the prince falsely as being responsible for Nyamewa's pregnancy. My mother suffered in the forest for many months until she finally met the old lady, who stayed with her, and catered for her till her *untimely* death. It was during my delivery that my mother passed on. So, I never saw my mother's face." Amambre narrated. There was loud silence after Amambre's story.

Nana Ekuntan, Ahenkan's father had died, and Ahenkan had succeeded him as chief of Esuekyir. Ahenkan himself was weak, and the then prince, Akroma, whom Ahenkan had later given birth to, was 'acting' in place of his father. No one knew the veracity of Amambre's story except Ahenkan. Ahenkan remembered Nyamewa, and knew that she had got pregnant for him but he thought she had been devoured by wild animals long ago. Amambre's story therefore *puzzled* him. He was petrified because he knew there was some consistency in Amambre's story. The elders of Esuekyir were even more confused about the whole narrative. Ahenkan *summoned* all the elders, including Akroma, his regent, and *disclosed* the truth to them. He *confessedly* informed his people that he indeed impregnated the poor girl, Nyamewa, but due to the *abominable* nature of the offence, he *connived* with his father to deny responsibility to the pregnancy. To authenticate their ploy, therefore, they carefully refuted Nyamewa and her father's claim, and put the father to death to make their stance look more serious and believable. They further threw the girl, Nyamewa, into the forest to *ostensibly* to rationalize their fiction. Ahenkan implored his elders to forgive him all his wrongdoings and believe Amambre's story.

"This is fake, it's spurious! This is *absurdity* won't be acceptable in this palace " some of the elders were heard *blurting out* angrily after the chief's submission. While some described it as *hallucination*, others thought the chief was under spirit possession. Others, however, *sympathized* with the tragic story of Nyamewa, and believed the chief. The *disgruntled* elders wondered how they would explain the chief's atrocities to the members of the community even if they believed him. They were even more *exasperated* that Ahenkan and his father had committed such *abominable* acts, and had *concealed* them all these years. They probed the chief's narrative further to *ascertain* the motive behind all those happenings. It was during the *probing* when Ahenkan revealed that he did all those things to protect the traditions of the land. According to their customs, anything that could potentially bring their traditional practices into disrepute had to be avoided at all costs. This meant that people had to use every means possible to protect the "stool" of the community, even if it required that one committed "the necessary evil". The elders were *speechless.* They were convinced that though the chief's conduct was unacceptable, it was the most *expedient* action to protect the "stool' from shame at that time. Ahenkan then stated that, to *compensate* Amambre for all the agony he had gone through due to he and his father's inactions, he should be installed a chief to succeed him. Just after this *confession*, Ahenkan passed on. The elders of Esuekyir couldn't *comprehend* the strange incidents that had revolved their "stool". They ended the meeting *abruptly* upon realizing the *demise* of their chief, and decided to meet the following day to take some *arbitrary* decisions. A message was sent to the queen mother, Obaapanyin Akua Assefoaba, about the death of the chief.

Early the following morning, the *Okomfo* visited the palace to perform some rituals that would empower the queen mother to *superintend* all the activities in the palace, especially, the processes to install a new chief.

After the *Okomfo's* visit, the elders met immediately to *deliberate* on the issues at hand. There were three main *agenda*; the discussion of the late chief's confession which was connected to Amambre's story, the discussion of the death of the chief which required that they *decapitated* three people, and buried them with the dead chief, and the preparation for the *installation* of a new chief, which had to be done before they could bury the *deceased* chief. Meanwhile, Amambre had been *confined* in a room with strict security at the entrance. The death of the chief was also kept among the elders of Esuekyir, given the many issues that had to be appropriated.

However, *as walls have always had ears*, Amambre's story had been heard by some community members. Those who were slaves from Amambre's mother's root and other neighboring communities were very happy about the turn of events. They had heard that Amambre had returned to pay his mother's "attackers" in their own coins. They swore to rally behind Amambre in his quest to revenge their opponents in the nick of time.

At the elders' meeting, tensions were high. The disagreement among them created three *factions* among the elders of Esuekyir. One faction, led by Opanyin

Essuman, *quashed* all the confessions of the late chief, and described Amambre's story as meaningless. They maintained that the chief might have suffered great mental disorder moments before his demise, and that, Amambre's story was a mere *fabricated coincidence*. According to them, accepting Amambre's story would create *irreparable distortions* in their traditions and customs. "If we believe the chief and Amambre, it means we have to perform many sacrifices to cleanse the entire stool, and find a way to compensate the *victims*, some of whom are not even alive. Why don't we stop crying over spilled milk?" they opined.

Another faction, led by Opanyin Ofori, stated that, they should ignore all those issues and install Akroma, Ahenkan's known son, as chief since, according to them, he had even acted as regent when his father was *bedridden*.

The third faction, led by Opanyin Apata, was of the view that, if they did not believe the chief and Amambre's stories, in order to correct the grievous harm done to those innocent people, the repercussions could be grave. They stressed that, those two stories narrated by the late chief and Amambre were *consistent*, and that the elders should not overlook.

These disputes got out of hand as they generated *pandemonium* among the elders. Soon, the uproar spread across the whole community with many explaining the incidents as *weird*, wild and wicked. Many native members of Esuekyir *bemoaned* that installing Ahenkan as chief in the first place was traditionally wrong, as according to them, it was the nephew of the chief who had to inherit the stool. It would, therefore, be another wrong practice if Ahenkan's supposed son, Amambre, was installed a chief, even if his story was *anything to go by*. They suggested that the stool should be taken to its original owners just to bury the hatchet.

CHAPTER SIX
THE ABRAFO LOOK FOR 'HUMAN HEAD' TO BURY WITH THE DEAD CHIEF

That night, the queen mother made the *gong-gong beater* announce to the entire community about the death of the chief, and the need for every parent to "protect" his or her children. No one was to go to farm for one week, neither should there be any noisemaking in the village. There shouldn't also be any pounding of fufu after six o'clock in the evening, nor any movement in the town at the same time. Any animal found *loitering* after six pm would be "seized".

That same night, the queen mother *summoned* the *Abrafo-* the *executioners*, to go on *human raid* to find three heads that would be buried with the late chief. These were all part of the practices of the community. Anytime a chief died, three people had to be killed and decapitated so that their heads would be buried with the dead chief. It was believed that those three persons would serve the chief in the *underworld*.

In the locked room, Amambre could overhear all the discussions about killing three people to "accompany" the dead chief. He was shocked to the marrow. He couldn't *fathom* how *unreasonable* some traditions could be. He believed all that the old lady had told him after hearing about that weird practice too. He got even more agitated to *emancipate* his people from the long *devastating* practices which he himself had suffered from. He however observed that, it would be a very difficult thing to do especially if he wanted to use dialogues. "The positions taken by the elders of the community wouldn't help matters at all," he reasoned. He vowed to do all he could to redeem his people from those unreasonable traditions, even if he had to sacrifice his life.

Early that dawn, the *Abrafo* went on the human raid whilst the elders also met to continue their *deliberations*. While the *Abrafo* made no "catch", the elders also couldn't reach any *consensus*. There were still divergent views about the installation of a new chief. They therefore adjourned their meeting to be continued the following day. The *Abrafo* also roamed from 2am till daybreak but did not get any "stray" person to arrest.

During the quiet hours of the afternoon the following day, the executioners went into the forest to continue their search. No one was to go to farm for a week so anyone met during those hours of the day would be considered a stray person. Such a person would be killed, and the head buried with the dead chief. This practice had continued for ages at Esuekyir. The four *Abrafo* roamed through the thick forest till nightfall but there was no sign of any human being to kill.

Tired and hungry, the executioners decided to return home. But they heard a strange conversation at a distance. They assembled quickly to ascertain the sound more clearly. They were convinced that the noise was coming from a woman and her children. The "conversation" implied that four people were involved. The *Abrafo* were in high hopes, thinking they had met their goal eventually. They scattered and walked stealthily towards the sound. Strangely, as they approached the sound, they heard it again at where they had just left. This continued for a while until a very strange and smelly wind started to blow around them. At that time, they sensed danger, but, the *Abrafo* were people who had been *immunized* spiritually against physical and spiritual attacks. They were immune to machete cuts, gunshots, and they could even "disappear" during extreme danger. Those potions in them made them extremely *fearsome* in human communities. Consequently, they laughed at, and *embraced* danger when in actual fact they should retreat.

They stuck their backs together, chewing the *Ogyamba* leaves, and making *incantations* when the strange smelly wind started blowing. *Ogyamba* is a tree in the forest whose herbs are used to scare and drive away evil spirits. Suddenly, however, a thorny and itchy rope tied them together. This was the time they had to vanish magically to avoid any *calamity* but unfortunately, they couldn't vanish because they could not plant their swords into the soil. They then heard a very strange voice sounding a strong warning that, they should believe the late chief's story and listen to Amambre. That voice echoed in their ears for a very long time, after which a swarm of bees strangely invaded them and beat them mercilessly. They *wailed* painfully, but no one could hear them from the thick forest.

After the bees had beaten them well enough, the rope tore, and the helpless executioners used their last strength to plant their swords into the soil, making them vanish *mysteriously* to appear in front of the palace.

Their sweaty bodies, together with the heavy swells on their skins attracted many people, who couldn't believe their sights for that bizarre scene. The elders, who had ended another meeting in total uproar, took to their heels upon seeing the "horror", with some falling vehemently, making many passers-by break into spontaneous laughter. Opanyin Ofori, who supported the installation of Akroma, other than Amambre, fell and somersaulted twice, and fell into the deep gutter behind the palace, *wramping* his spine. Though the falling of Opanyin Ofori into the gutter was *pitiful*, the manner with which he *somersaulted* from running too speedily for his age, created a lot laughter among the onlookers. His feeble screams from the gutter quickly attracted the energetic people around who sensed danger, to come to his aid.

The executioners couldn't talk to explain their ordeal to the queen mother and the other elders. They had lost their sense of speech. They could however, make signs that suggested that the people should believe the late chief and listen to Amambre. Their faces kept swelling from the bites of the bees, giving them very scary looks. That situation alarmed the queen mother and all the elders of the community, including the masses. Some people believed that Amambre might be an angry god who had come to take revenge on them. There were *murmurings* and *grumblings* everywhere in the community, with many blaming the late chief and the elders for committing and concealing atrocious deeds which had angered the gods to punish them that way.

Opanyin Ofori, who was the major opponent of the installation or Amambre as chief, became bedridden, and could not attend meetings at the palace anymore.

Fear gripped Akroma so much that, he couldn't comment on the chieftaincy issues again.

The Okomfo was invited to explain the strange happenings that had befallen the community but all he could say was how the executioners were tortured in the forest. He was asked whether the gods were unhappy with the people of Esueykir but he responded that he had not received any such information from the gods.

CHAPTER SEVEN
AMAMBRE BECOMES CHIEF OF ESUEKYIR

The responses of Okomfo Kuma *petrified* the people even more. They were thrown into despair. The executioners also died *successively* to the complete shock of everyone. At this juncture, the queen mother, Obaapanyin Ekua Assefoaba, realized that there was real danger. She was at her wit's end in her quest to understand those happenings, and to find solutions to them. To prevent any further damage, she ordered the release of Amambre and interrogated him the more. Amambre sounded serious, and his words carried some authority. Obaapanyin Ekua Assefoaba believed that even if Amambre's story was *unfounded*, it might be that nature wanted to correct certain things in their traditions and customs. She *convened* a meeting to initiate plans to install Amambre as the next chief of Esuekyir. Amambre was confined in the "study room" where supposed chiefs were taught the traditions and practices of the community, how to talk, walk and rule as a chief. Amambre seemed to know even more than his tutors.

He *demonstrated mastery* over their training. It came up that Amambre rather explained to his *tutors* the rationale behind most of their traditional practices, and how he intended to amend them if he were installed. His tutorials took eight days after which a date was fixed for his coronation.

Exactly one month after his tutorials, Amambre was *crowned* chief of Esuekyir. He constituted a new set of elders made up of some native members of Esuekyir and other members from different communities who had been captured as slaves. Some people however, disagreed with all those proceedings.

Amambre, met all the community members a week after his installation and disclosed his *philosophy* to them. He informed them that there were many practices that were against the *fundamental* human rights of the people, and had to be abolished. According to Amambre, customs and traditions were meant to develop the community by putting checks on the behaviour of the people, and not to harm. "All customs and traditions are meant for human good." Amambre explained that practices such as banishment or killing of people in the community for whatever offence, were barbaric , and had to be abolished. He narrated that if a woman were pregnant before going through the puberty rites, and the woman was killed or banished from the community, human life would be lost. If human life were lost, it affected the human resource development of the community. This, according to him, *retrogressed* the community, rather than developing it.

He questioned the wisdom behind the killing and the banishment of people from the community when life was more important than anything else in the world. Amambre maintained that there were more constructive ways of checking moral *decadence* in the community rather than those *outmoded* mechanisms. He didn't understand why the elders of the community didn't give themselves or their wards willingly to be killed and buried with their dead chiefs if indeed they wanted to serve their leaders. He *espoused* that, the zeal and the *reverence* with which they served their chiefs should be manifested in their readiness to die to accompany the dead chiefs so as to continue their service to them, instead of letting the Abrafo suffer through the forest to get some "stray people". "How could you let 'stray people' rather serve your dead chiefs? Why would you not let the royals do that job? He quizzed. Amambre revealed that all those practices were mere human *formulations*. They were not seconded by the ancestors nor the gods. "Nature is orderly and reasonable, it wouldn't do anything to harm humanity," he cajoled.

The community centre was as quiet as a cemetery during Amambre's *lecture*. His message did not only *enlighten* them, it puzzled them for the misery they had caused people ignorantly.

Amambre invited his elders and *outdoored* them to the community. He told them that his *administration* did not recognize slavery, and that, the days of wars were over. He announced that all slaves were free even to go back to their native villages. They were *at liberty* to return to their home communities and install their own chiefs. They could however, swear allegiance to them if they wished. All *confiscated* pieces of land were released to the owners. There was total happiness among the members of the community, especially, those who had been freed from captivity after many years of slavery. Some recounted how they had lost their relatives during the days of *imperialism*, and shed tears of joy. Whilst there was much merry making among many people, the other factions who were against the idea of Amambre becoming chief held secret meetings to overthrow and assassinate Amambre. They did not understand Amambre's "strange" laws. They believed that Amambre wasn't in to help, and that, he had changed their traditions to invoke the wrath of the gods and the ancestors.

CHAPTER EIGHT
ASSASSINS INVADE AMAMBRE'S PALACE

One Friday, four abled men invaded the palace. But for the timely *intervention* of Okyeame Kwesi Afer, who resisted the assassins fiercely, and screamed vehemently, the murderers would stab the chief, who was lying supine, alone in the palace. Amambre was awakened by the *scuffle* between Okyeame Kwesi Afer and the assassins, but, unfortunately, the linguist was stabbed to death by one of the attackers. The Chief woke up upon hearing the noise from the brawl, and ''scattered'' all of them.

He arrested them *single-handedly*, and unmasked them, exposing their faces to the public. People were shocked to see how some factions of the community had plotted such a thing, and had even killed *Okyeame* Kwesi Afer. They wondered why they couldn't let go of the *differences* after the queen mother, who was the overlord of the installation of chiefs, had even given her *consent.* The assassins were forced to mention all their *accomplices.* A special prison was constructed, and those criminals were thrown into it.

Okyeame Kwesi Afer was buried and a school was built in his honour. Due to his bravery and his protection of human life, the position of *Okyeame* was made a *bonafide* inheritance for his lineage. The first male children of his generation always occupied that position in the palace.

Amambre ruled with great might, wisdom and *justice*. His reign brought much development to the community in terms of *infrastructure*, and human resource. Today, Esuekyir is one of the most peaceful and advanced communities in Ghana.

MORAL

This novel describes some realities in our customs and traditions. It is believed that culture is dynamic, and must also be in the interest of the people. Culture should serve the common good of the masses. It is therefore imperative to examine and reexamine our cultural practices intermittently in order to discard the aspects which do not support modern development.

It is quite unwholesome to witness practices such as female genital mutilation, poor widowhood rites and witch camps still practised in some parts of Africa.

In some parts of Malawi, a man called 'hyena' is paid to have sex with girls at puberty as a form of 'ritual cleansing'. This implies that any girl who reaches puberty should have had sex with the 'hyena' in order to be rendered sexually clean, and acceptable in the community.

It is also an undisputed fact that some traditional Africans still kill people to be buried with dead chiefs.

The ritual killing of albinos and hunched backs are still practised in many parts of East Africa.

Trokosi, which denies girls of their right to education, is widely practised in some parts of the Volta Region of Ghana, some parts of Togo and Benin.

Though chastity is highly cherished among the Banyankole in Uganda, it against modern development to allow the aunt of a bride to sleep with the bridegroom, to ascertain his potency before the marriage is contracted. Checking a woman's virginity before marriage is however, commendable.

It is very clear that these practices are barbaric, inhuman, and flouts the fundamental human rites of the victims. They MUST THERFORE BE DISCARDED.

VOCABULARY

WORD   MEANING/ SYNONYMS

forefathers   ancestors, forebearers

invade	attack, encroach, enter by force
captors	jailers, kidnappers, arresters, nabbers
inhabitants	occupants, settlers, people who live in the place
spy	catch sight of, examine/watch/see secretly
alert	warn, signal, alarm, notify,
imminent	impending, immediate, inevitable, certain
fierce	extremely violent, very severe, ferocious, savage
devoured	killed, destroyed, greedily eaten
principles	rules, laws, guidelines
forbidden	prohibited, not allowed, illegitimate, unlawful

intimacy	relationship, intercourse , closeness
initiated	introduced, conferred membership
rigorous	intense, scrupulous, painstaking, strict
banished	sent away, expelled, driven away, ejected
taboos	things culturally forbidden from use, cultural prohibitions, cultural exclusions
paranormal	inexplicable, supernatural, pertaining to spirits/ghosts
phenomena	occurrences, events, issues, happenings
captive	prisoners, not free
ensued	occurred, resulted, took

	place
sprained	wramped, wrenched, weakened the joint of, dislocated
unquestionable	impeccable, undeniable, irrefutable,
apprenticeship	trade /craft learning,
native	born member, indigene, aboriginal, original member
notoriety	become infamous, ill-fame
undoubtedly	without doubts, unquestionably, undoubtably, doubtlessly, indubitably
infatuations	unreasoning love, sexual attractions, folly, unreasoning attachments

admired — esteemed, liked, approbated, liked

embarrass — humiliate, disgrace, abash, disconcert

genuine — real, true, pure, natural, not false

unequivocally — unambiguously, unmistakably, clearly,

flout — despise, disdain, reproach, break, scoff

lamented — bewailed, grieved, moaned, whined

sternly — harshly, unpleasantly, forbiddingly, dismally

hesitation — doubt, stammering, faltering,

disorganised — confused, shambolic,

disclose — uncover, reveal, unveil, divulge

consequences	aftercome, repercussions, results, aftermath
befall	happen to, occur
untoward	unfavourable, adverse, improper, disadvantageous
innocent	guiltless, blameless, free from guilt
contemplated	meditated on, pondered over, deliberated
affection	fondness, passion, attachment, love
distraught	saddened, worried, distressed, hurt
negotiate	come to terms, reach an agreement, confer, discuss
dilemma	undesirable circumstance, difficult problem, quandary, fix, pickle

kidnapped	seized/ detained unlawfully,
affair	adulterous relationship, intercourse
ruined	destroyed, wrecked, devastated
narrated	told, reported, recounted
uncontrollable	unbridle, too violent to be controlled
bragor	Akan term for puberty rites
anxious	worried, disturbed, restless, uneasy
proceedings	processes, procedures, measures, steps
adulthood	maturity, being an adult
courageous	brave, bold, hardy, valorous

queried	questioned, inquired, quizzed
compounded	increased, worsened, aggravated
established	found out, discovered, ascertained
grievous	dreadful, dire, awful, terrible, dismal, horrible
whispered	hinted, rumoured, said feebly
vehemently	intensely, forcefully, passionately
oblivious	unaware, unmindful, forgetful, ignorant
inescapable	unavoidable, certain
concocted	contrived, schemed, plotted, invented
repercussions	consequences, aftereffects,

	results
damning	condemning, damaging
fury	anger, indignance, resentment
precarious	perilous, dangerous, unsafe
allegation	accusation,
abominable	abhorrence, odious, hateful, loathsome
traduced	defamed, denigrated, besmirched
explicitly	clearly, expressly, specifically
plausible	credible, meaningful, acceptable
specious	deceitful, fallacious, insincere, meretricious
drenched	completely wet, sodden,

	soaked
dumbfounded	speechless, bewildered, confused,
ingenuity	cleverness, ingenuousness
denigrating	disrepute, discredit, traduce, disparage, defame
destination	place, venue
grieved	worried, mourned, lamented, wept
predecessors	forerunners, foregangers, forefathers
atrocities	enormous wickedness, extreme criminalities/ cruelties
sobbed	cried, wept with convulsive gasps
hiccupping	spasm

escapades	adventures,
immune	protected, not susceptible
exhume	take out, unbury, disinter
concoction	medicine, mixture
identity	selfhood, individuality, personality,
marveled	wondered, watched with astonishment/shock/dismay
verbal	oral, in words, spoken
labour	giving birth, childbirth, delivery
due	up
curiosity	inquisitiveness
logs	trunks of trees, pieces of timber
catchment	river basin, area liable to

	flood
randomly	without direction, vehemently, forcefully
aftermath	effects, consequences
subsided	calmed, abated, became tranquil, eased
downstream	lower part of the stream
colostrum	beestings, foremilk
weaned	ceased giving milk to
coined	made, fabricated, invented, originated
centuries	hundreds of years, a very long time
adventures	dangerous expeditions, risky encounters
counter	contrary, opposing, opposite

spurious	false, illegitimate, counterfeit, bogus, unauthentic , fallacious, baseless
lineage	descent, progeny, race,
strangle	choke, suffocate, throttle
offspring	baby, little one, progeny
reasoned	thought, considered, deduced,
consciousness	self awareness, witfulness,
perpetrators	orchestrators, masterminds, people responsible
heinous	reprehensible, abominable, horrible, odious
constructive	productive, helpful
misdemeanour	petty crime, minor offence

admonished	warned, reprimanded, chided, counselled, reproved
propositions	ideas, proposals, suggestions, considerations
dialogue	discuss, negotiate, discourse, liaise
abolish	cancel, revoke, dissolve, repeal, abrogate, annul
inhuman	cruel, barbaric, heartless
opposition	antagonism, hatred
resilient	enduring, strong, determined, persistent
antagonist	opponent, enemy, adversary, rival
misconceptions	mistaken beliefs, wrong ideas

inept	unfit, incompetent, impotent
benediction	blessing
inheritance	that which he is entitled to inherit
approached	drew closer to, got/went nearer to
reverberating	ringing, echoing, sounding repeatedly
commensurate	proportionate , equal in measure
splash	plash, sound
squealed	screamed, shrilled, wailed
darted	moved quickly, rushed, hurried
apparently	clearly, evidently, manifestly
considerable	significant, appreciable

herblore	knowledge in herbs, herbalism,
herbalism	knowledge in medicinal herbs, herblore
current	flow
recalled	remembered, recollected,
bizarre	strange, unusual, odd
resuscitated	regained consciousness,
reverence	respect, awe, zeal
ambushment	waylay, attack unexpectedly
sandwiched	put between two others and moved
formulations	compositions, make ups, constitutions
sumptuous	delicious, very tasty, splendid

stemmed	came, were derived, originated, emanated
untimely	premature, early, unexpected
outmoded	old-fashioned, unfashionable, antiquated, out of date, backward
espoused	opined
puzzled	confused, perplexed, bewildered,
summoned	invited, called, assembled, convoked
confessedly	admittedly
ostensibly	seemingly, apparently
connived	conspired, colluded, schemed
absurdity	logical contradiction, implausibility,

	dubiousness
blurting out	shouting inconsiderately, uttering suddenly, speaking quickly without thought
hallucination	delusions, delirium tremens
sympathized	had a common feeling, empathised
disgruntled	dissatisfied, frustrated, unhappy
exasperated	greatly annoyed, furious
concealled	hidden, kept secret, mithed
ascertain	find out, discover, establish, determine
probing	investigating, exploring, questioning

speechless	dumbfounded, confounded, silent due to amazement
expedient	proper, suitable,
compensate	indemnify, satisfy, remunerate, appease, reward
confession	open admittance, open admission
comprehend	understand, grasp, perceive
abruptly	suddenly, without notice, unceremoniously
demise	death
arbitrary	impulsive, random
superintend	oversee, supervise
agenda	issues, matters, worklists, dockets

decapitated	beheaded, decollate, removed the head
installation	crowning, setting up
factions	divisions, groups
quashed	rejected, disapproved
fabricated	made-up, manufactured, cooked up, invented
coincidence	occurrence at the same time
irreparable	incurable, unamendable,
distortions	deformities, contortions, perversions
victims	sufferers, offended, disadvantaged
bedridden	confined to bed due to illness
	compatible, accordant, agreeable, conformable,

consistent	harmonious
pandemonium	chaos, violence, uproar, confusion, outburst
weird	strange, creepy, eerie, odd
bemoaned	bewailed, complained, moaned
loitering	roaming, gallivanting
executioners	people who execute capital punishment
underworld	the world of the dead, afterlife, netherworld
gong-gong beater	someone who beats a gong to disseminate information in local villages
fathom	grasp, find out the meaning
unreasonable	meaningless, arbitrary

emancipate	free, liberate, redeem
devastating	damaging, ruining,
deliberations	discussions, considerations
consensus	agreement
immunized	inoculated, vaccinated, protected
fearsome	frightening, terrifying, scary, awful, terrible
embraced	welcomed, hugged
incantations	magical recitals
calamity	disaster, catastrophe, ruin
wailed	cried, howled, screamed painfully
mysteriously	strangely, inexplicably
wramping	spraining, wrenching, twisting

Word	Meaning
pitiful	sad, sorrowful, eliciting pity
somersaulted	rotated, rolled, tumbled
grumblings	complaints, murmurings, rumblings
murmurings	complaints, grumblings
petrified	extremely scared, frightened
successively	in turns, one after the other,
unfounded	baseless, groundless, ungrounded
convened	summoned, convoked, called together
demonstrated	displayed, showed, exhibited
mastery	command, expertise, skill, great prowess

tutors	teachers, instructors, lecturers
crowned	installed, enstooled, coronated
philosophy	ideologies, belief system, thoughts, worldview
fundamental	basic, primary, elementary
retrogressed	retarded, declined the progress of, brought backwards
decadence	decay, deterioration, decline
lecture	exposition, teaching, speech
enlighten	furnish with knowledge, brighten the intellect
outdoored	unveiled, inaugurated
administration	governance, reign, office

confiscated	seized, claimed, conquered
imperialism	territorial dominance, invasions
intervention	interference, coming in
scuffle	struggle, fight, , wrestle
single-handedly	alone, without help from others
differences	disagreements, arguments, disputes, dissensions
consent	approval, assent, permission
accomplices	allies, assistants, abettors, associates
bona fide	genuine, authentic, legitimate
justice	fairness, impartiality,
infrastructure	basic facilities

play to their weaknesses   *take
advantage of their weaknesses*
passed away   *died, passed on,
kicked the bucket*
catered for   *took care of,
looked after*
took care of   *catered for,
looked after*
single-handedly   *alone, without
the help of others*
dos and don'ts   *rules and
regulations*
have his way   *to do what one
wants to do especially,*   *to have sexual
affair*
came across   *met, found ,
usually by accident*
bumped into   *met by chance*
well-mannered   *polite, having
good behaviour, well-behaved*
under a cloud   *disgraced/
lost trust*
let me be   *leave me
alone, do not disturb me,*

unyielding   dogmas
practices/beliefs which are not profitable
pour oil into flames   make the
already bad situation worse, aggravate the
situation
take the rough with the smooth   to accept
the unpleasant part of a situation as well
as the

pleasant part
through with   finished
with
at their wit's end   have
reached their mental or emotional
limitations
drag the traditions of the land through the
mud   tarnish or spoil the
reputation of the

stoop   so   low
moral standards too high to do something
unpleasant
no need to cry over spilled milk
doesn't have to worry about something in
the past that

can't be changed
as   walls   have   always   had   ears
someone might be eavesdropping
anything   to   go   by
something to be take seriously/ used as an
example
at liberty   free,
entitled, allowed
 catch a glimpse of   catch
sight of, I have a look at, watch